THE TWELVE DAYS OF CHRISTMAS

THE TWELVE DAYS OF CHRISTMAS

Laurel Long

PUFFIN BOOKS

an imprint of Penguin Group (USA)

PUFFIN BOOKS
Published by the Penguin Group
Penguin Group (USA) LLC
375 Hudson Street
New York, New York 10014

USA * Canada * UK * Ireland * Australia
New Zealand * India * South Africa * China

penguin.com
A Penguin Random House Company

First published in the United States of America by Dial Books, an imprint of Penguin Group (USA) Inc.
Published by Puffin Books, an imprint of Penguin Young Readers Group, 2014

Copyright © 2011 by Laurel Long
Sheet music provided by Musicnotes.com. Copyright © 2009 Musicnotes, Inc.
All rights reserved.
Music composition by Bob Sherwin.

THE LIBRARY OF CONGRESS HAS CATALOGED THE DIAL EDITION AS FOLLOWS:
Long, Laurel.
The twelve days of Christmas / Laurel Long.
p. cm.
Summary: An illustrated version of the traditional song.
ISBN 978-0-8037-3357-2 (hardcover)
1. Folk songs, English—England—Texts. 2. Christmas music—Texts. [1. Folk songs—England.
2. Christmas music.] I. Title.PZ8.3.L85Tw 2009 782.42—dc22 2008015774

Puffin Books ISBN 978-0-14-751286-4

The art for the book was created using oil paints.

1 3 5 7 9 10 8 6 4 2

For Sara

On the first day of Christmas,
My true love gave to me
A partridge in a pear tree.

On the second day of Christmas,
My true love gave to me
Two turtle doves,
And a partridge in a pear tree.

On the third day of Christmas,
My true love gave to me
Three French hens,
Two turtle doves,
And a partridge in a pear tree.

4

On the fourth day of Christmas,
My true love gave to me
Four collie birds,
Three French hens,
Two turtle doves,
And a partridge in a pear tree.

On the fifth day of Christmas,
My true love gave to me
Five golden rings,
Four collie birds,
Three French hens,
Two turtle doves,
And a partridge in a pear tree.

6

On the sixth day of Christmas,
My true love gave to me
Six geese a-laying,
Five golden rings,
Four collie birds,
Three French hens,
Two turtle doves,
And a partridge in a pear tree.

On the seventh day of Christmas,
My true love gave to me
Seven swans a-swimming,
Six geese a-laying,
Five golden rings,
Four collie birds,
Three French hens,
Two turtle doves,
And a partridge in a pear tree.

On the eighth day of Christmas,
My true love gave to me
Eight maids a-milking,
Seven swans a-swimming,
Six geese a-laying,
Five golden rings,
Four collie birds,
Three French hens,
Two turtle doves,
And a partridge in a pear tree.

On the ninth day of Christmas,
My true love gave to me
Nine ladies dancing,
Eight maids a-milking,
Seven swans a-swimming,
Six geese a-laying,
Five golden rings,
Four collie birds,
Three French hens,
Two turtle doves,
And a partridge in a pear tree.

10

On the tenth day of Christmas,
My true love gave to me
Ten lords a-leaping,
Nine ladies dancing,
Eight maids a-milking,
Seven swans a-swimming,
Six geese a-laying,
Five golden rings,
Four collie birds,
Three French hens,
Two turtle doves,
And a partridge in a pear tree.

On the eleventh day of Christmas,
My true love gave to me
Eleven pipers piping,
Ten lords a-leaping,
Nine ladies dancing,
Eight maids a-milking,
Seven swans a-swimming,
Six geese a-laying,
Five golden rings,
Four collie birds,
Three French hens,
Two turtle doves,
And a partridge in a pear tree.

On the twelfth day of Christmas,
My true love gave to me
Twelve drummers drumming,
Eleven pipers piping,
Ten lords a-leaping,
Nine ladies dancing,
Eight maids a-milking,
Seven swans a-swimming,
Six geese a-laying,
Five golden rings,
Four collie birds,
Three French hens,
Two turtle doves,
And a partridge in a pear tree!

A PARTRIDGE IN A PEAR TREE • TWO TURTLE DOVES
NINE LADIES DANCING • TEN LORDS A-LEAPING
ELEVEN PIPERS PIPING • TWELVE DRUMMERS DRUMMING

THE TWELVE DAYS

OF CHRISTMAS English Traditional Carol

Artist's Note

The Twelve Days of Christmas has mysterious origins and hidden meanings. One thing is certain: The days are the twelve festive days that begin on Christmas Day when Jesus was born and end on the Epiphany when the three Magi visited him, culminating in the Twelfth Night feast.

"The Twelve Days of Christmas" was first published as a children's book called *Mirth Without Mischief* in England in 1780. However, there are three older versions. It is thought to have originated in France as a possible Twelfth Night memory game. The players would repeat previous verses and add one more. If a player made an error, he or she would have to give a kiss or a gift to someone else.

The phrase "a partridge in a pear tree" gives some evidence of the song's transition from its French origins. The pear tree is actually a *perdrix*, French for partridge and pronounced *per-dree*. The word was copied down incorrectly when the oral version of the game was transcribed from French to English. The original line would have been: *A partridge, une perdrix*. Another change to the original is the modern usage of *calling birds*, whereas the original line was four collie (or colly) birds, referring to common blackbirds. In England a coal mine is called a colliery and colly or collie means black like coal.

There are many interpretations of the song's lyrics. One suggestion is that "The Twelve Days of Christmas" was a Christian song with secret references to the teachings of the faith, perhaps dating from the sixteenth century religious wars in England. For example, some say that the lords a-leaping symbolized the Ten Commandments. However, the British believe that the ten lords a-leaping were Moorish dancers who performed during the Christmas feast.

The questions surrounding the history and symbolism of "The Twelve Days of Christmas" open it up to a variety of artistic approaches. My interpretation of "The Twelve Days of Christmas" is a visual story that contains two mysteries. The first is the mystery of the hidden images. The second mystery is a visual one that takes the reader through the days and seasons of a world that only exists in the tower shown on day 11. On day 12, the angels enter the tower through the Christmas wreath. In the last illustration, the world inside the tower is shown complete with all of the scenes and characters as they are depicted throughout the book. In this way, the animals could be inside and protected from the windy, winter cold and still be shown enjoying the flowered fields and flowing streams of the outdoors.

This version of "The Twelve Days of Christmas" is also about the passage of time and the order and mystery of life with all of its certainties and surprises. Time is defined by the twelve days, the twelve months, and the twelve hours on a clock. The repetition of the song's lyrics mimic the repeating cycles of the seasons, the turns of the hands on a clock, the phases of the moon around the sun, and the dawn and dusk of each day.

L OOK CLOSELY AND YOU'LL FIND THAT THERE ARE
TREASURES SECRETLY HIDDEN WITHIN EACH PICTURE.

1 = PARTRIDGE	5 = GOLDEN RING	9 = LADY DANCING
2 = TURTLE DOVE	6 = GEESE	10 = LORD A-LEAPING
3 = FRENCH HEN	7 = SWAN	11 = PIPER
4 = COLLIE BIRD	8 = MAID A-MILKING	12 = DRUMMER

SEE IF YOU CAN FIND THEM ALL!

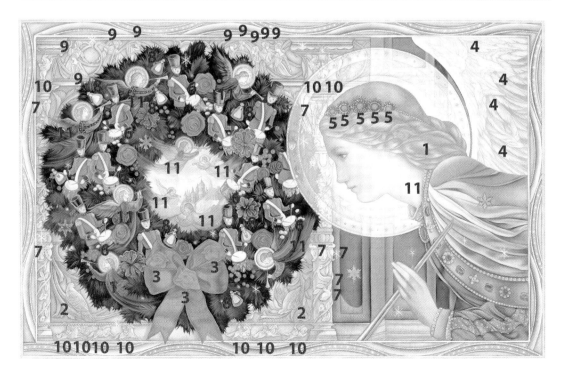